Contents

CW01023993

Narrator's note: Burt the badger speaks with a lisp.

Credits

I would like to personally thank Hannah Oliver, Riley's mum, for asking me to write my first children's book for my grandson, Riley Oliver Walton.

Riley meets Frupp

It was a blisteringly hot summer's day in the friendly town of Windowsill Ledge, where Riley lived. There was hardly a breeze, and because the temperature had been so high for the last five weeks, the tarmac on the roads had begun to melt and the train tracks had started to buckle and twist in the heat of the sun.

There was a water shortage too, and you couldn't use your garden hose to water your plants. It was so dry that lorries had to deliver it to every street in the town, and the outdoor swimming pool was full up with people trying to keep cool.

This was how the last week of Riley's summer holiday began. He was hot, bothered and just a tiny bit bored. Dad was at work, mum was busy in the kitchen, and most of his friends were away on holiday. It was then that he decided to visit his grandad's allotment for the first time by himself. He took a drink and a snack bar, and he was ready for his first adventure.

Grandad's allotment was just up the road from Riley's house, and when he arrived it was strangely silent, too quiet in fact. There were no crackling fires or chatter from the other shed owners, just the noises from the animals and the birds that lived rent-free in Twizzy Wood nearby. He thought that he was alone, but was he?

Riley made his way to grandad's shed, but found it was locked up. Then he remembered that he was away on his canal boat. So he went for a walk into the wood, where it was wild and overgrown, cool and shady, but just a little bit scary.

He wandered around looking for something to do, and found a long stick which he threw around like a spear for a while. Then, further into the wood, he saw a huge oak tree with one long sturdy branch sticking out from it. Someone had thrown a piece of rope over it and had tied it to an old tractor tyre.

After swinging to and fro on it a number of times, Riley decided to make things a bit more exciting. He stood up on the big tyre. This way he found he could swing a lot higher. He was just enjoying the view when he slipped and began to fall from a great height towards the biggest clump of stinging nettles he had ever seen!

He was within inches of being stung to bits by the stingy stinging nettles when a spindly branch wrapped itself around his waist and dropped him safely onto the ground.

Confused by his escape from harm, Riley looked around to see who or what had saved him. Then he heard a quiet voice say, "Hey, hi, I'm Frupp Twizzy. What's your name?" Riley couldn't see anyone at first and blurted out, "What..., how..., where are you?" "My name's Riley, I still can't see you." "Don't be scared," Frupp said calmly, "I'm standing between the two trees in front of you."

Riley looked around, but still couldn't see who was talking to him. "No," Frupp said, "you're looking for a human, aren't you?" Riley replied sharply. "Well of course I am," still not sure what was going on. "Well, I'm not human you see, I'm..., I'm a young tree. Hang on I'll wave my branches." Frupp added.

And there, right in front of Riley, stood a small tree. It had a face, of sorts, thin branches for arms, thicker ones for legs and a stocky trunk and its feet were made of roots! Well, Riley's gob had never been so smacked, especially as he could see that Frupp could walk!

Riley was full of questions such as, “Where did you come from? How did you end up living here?” And, “How come you’re called Frupp?”

“Whoa, slow down there,” Frupp said! “You see those two oak trees, the ones that are wrapped around each other?” “That’s my mum and dad.” And sure enough, when Riley looked a little further into the wood, there were two oak trees, one taller than the other. “They started life as two single trees and over time they grew together.” Frupp added.

“How did I get here,” Frupp added? “How did you end up living in a house,” he asked Riley? “Oh, that’s easy,” he said, “I lived in mum’s tummy for nine months first.” “Ewwww gross,” Frupp remarked in alarm! “Tell me about it,” Riley said, “it was like living inside a bubble.

“So how were you born, Riley asked?” “Well,” Frupp replied, “dad said that it involved lots of flashing lights, a big bang, and then a crashing sound! It was a dark and stormy night apparently,” Frupp went on, “the rain was beating down and the wind was howling and blowing through the trees in the wood. Every shed on the allotment began to shake and rattle and, way off in the distance a big thunderstorm was building up; frapp, fripple and frupple the thunder went, as it echoed through the air.”

“The clouds got bigger and darker and thicker and then lightning began to shoot across the sky in all directions, flash and flicker it went, flicker and flash.”

“The lightning moved closer and closer to the allotment, and one bolt struck the corner of a shed and part of it collapsed with a crash! All went quiet for a while. Then, out of nowhere, one enormous bolt of lightning flashed its way across the sky and it was heading for the trees in Twizzy Wood.”

“As it shot to down to the ground at the speed of well, lightning I guess, it hit dad. He was protecting mum at the time, and I dropped off one of her branches in 2009. Dad lost his favourite branch, but they both survived the strike. I was just a tiny acorn then, but pretty soon after that I grew into a sapling. Dad says he’s glad he’s not a horse chestnut tree as their conkers drop off once a year!”

“And my name?” Frupp asked. “Well, why are you called Riley?” They both stared into each other’s eyes searching for an answer and then said together laughing, “Because that’s what mum and dad called us!”

“What about food?” Riley asked. “What do you eat?” “Well,” Frupp replied, “if I’m hungry I just put my feet into a puddle and suck up some water. The sun is good for me too, it helps me to grow – that’s all I really need.” “What about you

Riley, what do you eat," Frupp asked? "Oooh loads of stuff me," Riley explained, "breakfast, dinner and tea, but what I really like most of all is... sweets!"

"So," Riley said building up to more questions, "how long have you lived here?" Frupp asked. "Let's see, mum and dad are really, really old now and can't speak to humans, or walk about like me. They're over 30 years old, I think, and I'm seven, so... seven years then." "Wow," Riley said, "we're the same age!"

"And how come you've got a nest where your tummy should be," Riley asked, pointing at the hole in Frupp's stomach? "Knot 'oles," Frupp said with a smirk. "And the same to you," Riley replied with a grin! "You think this is odd," Frupp added? "Dads got bats in his trunk!" "You get bats in your trunks, gosh I bet that's uncomfortable," Riley said giggling to himself!

"You've got a strange sense of humour," Frupp said. "You think I'm strange, just wait until you meet my grandad," Riley said. "He's as daft as a box of frogs!"

"All trees have knotholes," Frupp went on, "and sometimes squirrels chew on them and make homes for themselves, or woodpeckers peck at them and make nests. You see, here in the wood, we all help each other out." "Hmmm, I see," Riley said, "sounds like a good place to be."

"You've got some funny looking bark too, it's all soft and squidgy," Frupp said, prodding at the skin on Riley's face with one of his branches. "And what are you wearing," he asked inquisitively? "That's skin you plum," Riley said, "and these are called clothes."

"Look, I've got trainers and socks on and a pair of shorts, plus a T shirt too." "Well, what are those things called," Frupp asked, pointing at the sleeves? "Arm 'oles," Riley replied. "And the same to you," Frupp said with a grin.

"You speak well for a tree," Riley said. "Well, I should do, I am an English oak," Frupp said. "Oh yes, so you are," Riley added. "So, what's the name of your school?" "Barking High," Frupp replied, "get it, Barking!" "Very funny," Riley said.

Then he added, "Well I'd better be off home before mum explodes, she doesn't know where I am." "You mean your mum goes off bang," Frupp said in surprise? "Ha, I'll tell you about that the next time I see you, tomorrow probably," Riley said laughing.

Frupp waddled back to join his mum and dad and Riley made his way back down the muddy path, past the sheds and the drippy taps and headed for home.

He felt as though he'd made an odd, but a new friend. Could he tell his mum and dad and friends? No! This was the Twizzy Wood secret between him and Frupp, and he was looking forward to his next adventure down at grandad's allotment.

As he walked past a large clump of bushes, one of the branches moved downwards, upwards and downwards again. This was because standing behind one bush was... a stranger! He had dark scary eyes and was wearing a dark hat, dark clothes and thick black boots – oooh, very spooky!

The naughty barbed wire incident

When Riley set out on his next adventure he took his bike with him, as he nearly got caught out the last time when he arrived home late. Dad was at work and it was mum's day off and, as she was giving their home an early spring clean, Riley knew that she would be busy for ages. This was his cue to leave for the allotment.

The sun was out, but there was no sign of Frupp, just a couple of people working on their plots of land at the top of the allotment when he arrived. Riley rode up and down for a while and soon began to get bored, so he decided to build a ramp for his bike so that he could jump over it and skid to a halt in the dirt.

He found some bricks near grandad's shed, and a long plank of wood at the back of the shed next door and began building his take-off platform. After stacking the bricks on top of each other at one end the plank, he was almost ready to try it out.

Riley made sure that he had enough space to jump in the air and room to stop and skid to a halt without hitting anything – or so he thought. He mounted his bike and prepared for his first proper jump.

Down he went towards the ramp, building up speed as he pedalled as fast as he could. He hit the end of the ramp at a tremendous speed, shot up the length of the plank and was soon flying high in the air.

Just then, the branches moved up and down on a tree to the left of Riley, and he just caught a glimpse of a dark figure that was lurking in the shadows. It was..., shock, horror and gasp..., the stranger again!

Riley saw him out of the corner of his eye, which seemed very, very odd to him as he thought that both of his eyes were round!

The surprise of seeing the stranger had badly affected Riley's sense of balance, and he and his bike began to wobble in mid-air, wobble-obble-obble they went. He hit the ground with a thump, slammed on the brakes and then began to skid out of control. He was now heading for a collision with one of grandad's friends shed, who he called 'Hardly-Ever', and he couldn't stop no matter how hard he tried!

In the blink of an eye Riley saw a huge pile of grass cuttings, which he thought would make a soft-landing place if he came off of his bike, but time had run out for that idea. He crashed into the corner of Hardly-Ever's shed, skidded to the right and landed, head first, into a pile of dead leaves instead.

"Oh my gosh that hurts," Riley said after he spat out the leaves from his mouth. When the dust and leaves had settled, he could see and feel that he hadn't got away with his landing unharmed.

When he brushed off the scattered leaves from his bike, he could see that his chain had come off and was now wrapped around his right ankle. Unfortunately, this was only half of his problem.

On top of Hardly-Ever's shed was a large roll of nasty, spikey and very, very rusty barbed wire, which grandad said that he'd kept in case another war started!

When Riley hit the shed, he'd knocked a support post away that kept it level. And now it was three inches shorter at one end and the slope was just enough to make the barbed wire begin to roll down the roof slowly towards where Riley was sitting!

Frupp was dozing in the sun, but woke up when he heard the sound of the crash. He could see the danger that Riley was in, but he couldn't get there fast enough to stop another accident. Now was the time to call on his friends for some help.

He waved his branches and called out for Furkitt the Frog, but he couldn't save Riley by himself either, so Furkitt alerted Petunia the pigeon by jumping up and down on his lily pad in the allotment's pond shouting, "Oi oi, braaap-braaap flipping braaap-braaap." Which, as I'm sure you know in frog language means, "'elp flipping 'elp, flipping 'elp, 'elp!"

The nervous cockney pigeon said what she always said in times of trouble, "Ooh my Gawd, I just can't cope, it'll all end in tears." And then sprang into action.

She flew high into the air right up to the top of a beech tree where she knew some magpies lived and cooed out loudly, "Coo-blimey, coo-flippin' 'eck, can you give us an 'and?" "Sure," said Max the head of the magpies, "what's afoot?" "It's that thin dangly thing at the end of your leg, but that's not important right now, Frupp's friend Riley is in danger," Petunia said hurriedly.

"Okay, I'll alert my squadron," Max said reassuringly. In no time at all, he'd assembled his fastest and strongest fliers. As they ran through their flight checks for take-off, they waited to hear the news of their mission.

Just then Magpie Air Traffic Control sent this message to Max and the rest of the squadron. "Weather's looking fine, you're clear for take-off." "Roger Control," Max replied, and with that they all took to the sky.

As the squadron flew over the allotment, Max got on the radio to explain the situation to them. "Okay chaps, lock onto Hardly-Ever's shed, human boy in danger, barbed wire roll about to drop on his head, bike chain caught around ankle, over and out."

Well, Frupp, Furkitt and Petunia had done everything in their power to help. All they could do now was sit back and watch the rescue plan unfold.

Riley lay there tangled up in his bike, still in quite a lot of pain, totally unaware of the danger that he was still in, but help was on its way. Max had a plan fixed in his mind and passed this message onto the squadron.

"Listen up chaps, what we need," he said, "is one long dead branch or an old fencepost and two pieces of thick string. Peel off in pairs, see what you can find." "Roger leader," the squadron replied. And with that they split up to search for the items that Max had mentioned.

A few moments later Magpies 2 and 3 reported back to Max. "String at 6 o'clock, fencepost at 4 o'clock leader, what's the plan?" Max replied, "Split up lads, swoop down and wrap a piece of string around each end of the fencepost. Magpies 3 and 4, get ready to follow them."

"Your mission," Max added, "is to pick up the ends of the rope with Magpies 2 and 3 and fly over the shed dropping the fencepost in front of the barbed wire, I'll take care of the bike chain." And remarkably his plan was a total success.

Max said jubilantly, "Spot on chaps well done, let's head for home, worms and medals all round I think." And with that they disappeared back to their nests.

By this time Riley had realised his lucky escape and Frupp, Furkitt and Petunia went over to see how he was. "Thanks guys," he said, "can you thank the magpies for me," Riley asked? "Sure," Petunia said. "No problem, that's what friends are for."

Pointing at Furkitt and Petunia, Riley said, "I take it that these two are friends of yours?" "They sure are," Frupp replied with a smile. "Wow," Riley said, "this place gets more and more interesting by the day!" "You just wait until you meet the rest of us," Furkitt said. Riley said in surprise, "You mean there are more of you?" "Oh yes," Petunia added, we've got quite a gang here.

Riley added, "I've got a question, how come grandad calls the owner of this shed Hardly-Ever?" And Furkitt replied, "Oh that's easy, he's hardly ever here!" "Oh Furkitt," Petunia said raising her eyebrows. Furkitt added with a grin, "Hey, don't look at me, it's Riley's daft grandad who named him that!"

Riley said goodbye to his new friends and began to make his way home. He cycled down the muddy path and through the open three bar gate and out onto the road. He couldn't wait to return to the allotment the next day to meet more of Frupp's friends. Even so, he was still keeping an eye out for the mysterious stranger!

Riley nearly gets the chop!

It was the first day of Riley's summer holiday that the sun hadn't come out. The sky was overcast and the wind was picking up nicely too. That didn't bother him though, he was heading off to the allotment no matter what the weather was doing.

On his way there he was laughing to himself, as his dad and grandad were always making up odd names for things and people. And grandad had nicknames for most of the shed owners that used the allotment.

There was 'Dustpan-Ann' for starters. She was always walking around with a brush in her hand, but didn't have a dustpan to go with it! And there was a man that grandad called 'Cuffed it', because every time he spoke, he rubbed his nose on his shirt sleeves! Riley didn't understand all of grandad's jokes or the silly names that he called people, but his dad said that he would when he got a bit older.

It would turn out to be a strange old day. A day full of surprises and unseen danger again. As Riley walked by 'Pullover Pete's' shed he noticed that his door was wide open, but Pete, another friend of grandad's, was nowhere to be seen.

As he'd left his jacket at home, Riley went inside to shelter from the wind. When he looked around, he saw a lot of tools hanging up, and there was one really large one that caught his eye leaning against the wall at back of the shed.

Massive it was, with a long odd-shaped wooden handle. It must have been at least two feet taller than Riley, and on the end of it was a long sharp curved blade.

What he'd found was a scythe and it was used for cutting down long grass and crops back in the old days. Riley remembered grandad telling him about the sharp tool and said that he should never touch it, as it was really, really dangerous.

But Riley was an inquisitive boy, and he couldn't resist dragging it outside to have a proper look at it, and he tried to pick it up. He soon realised though that it was too heavy, so he leant it up against the outside of Pullover's shed to the left of the door frame for a while.

Then, rather than leave the blade on the ground, where people might trip over it, Riley used a hole in the ground at the front of the shed to prop the scythe up. But this left the blade resting at the top of the door frame with the point of the scythe facing towards him. Now it was in a more dangerous position than it was before!

While Riley was thinking about what to do next, he sat down next to a box of water melons, which was outside of the shed and began playing a game on his phone.

He remembered grandad saying that he'd bought an i-phone once, but he had to take it back to the shop. He told the lady behind the counter that he couldn't hear anything with his eye, and asked for an ear-phone instead!

It was then that the stranger appeared again! He hadn't been seen for a while, but there was no doubt about it, it did look as if he was keeping his beady eyes on Riley for some reason. And, as usual, he was hiding in the shadows of the trees and bushes wearing dark clothing and his big black boots.

Just then Norman the gnat, Norm to his friends, went buzzing by. There were always a lot of gnats around Pullover Pete's plot of land, mainly because he grew a lot of fruit, and gnats love fruit. Norm was another friend of Frupp's and he's a bit well, whizzy-whizzy-buzz-buzz, and seemed to enjoy flying around in circles.

As he flew past, he saw Riley and where he'd left the scythe and thought to himself, "That looks like an accident waiting to happen." So, he went in search of someone bigger than himself to help if something did go wrong.

Frupp was nowhere to be seen. But, underneath the decking at the bottom of 'Bean Pole's' shed, a neighbour of grandad's, Norm noticed the yellow waistcoat and the tip of the tail of a dozing Loxly Fox flicking up and down in his den. All Norm had to do now was find a way of waking him up.

As Riley could be in danger, sooner rather than later, Norm felt it was time for some swift action. He flew back about 20 feet from where Loxly was snoozing and prepared himself for a high-speed, long-range attack.

He whizzed about and flapped his wings with all of his might and seconds later he shot straight up Loxly's left nostril and out again, and his trick worked!

Loxly woke up from his slumber, and after squinting his eyes, letting out a long yawn and sneezing twice he said to Norm, "Oh hallo old boy, how can I help?" And Norm told him about the danger that Riley might be in.

Loxly Foxa

"Well," Loxly said lazily, "I suppose we'd better saunter over there and see what's what and decide on a rescue plan if we need it." And with that they both made their way over to Pullover's shed. Loxly crept quietly along in the shadows of the trees and bushes, while Norm flapped and buzzed urgently trying to keep up with him.

Meanwhile, Riley who'd got bored with the game on his phone, was standing over the box that contained the large water melons and was trying to pick up the top one.

He'd managed to lift it up a little way, but as it was so big and so heavy, he dropped it back down with a thud and the shed shook a little. Loxly and Norm looked at each other and could see what may happen and began to hatch a rescue plan.

The level of danger moved up a notch when a gust of wind blew over the allotment, and the scythe rattled against the side of the shed and moved a little closer towards Riley! Fortunately, a rusty nail stopped it falling any further!

*[Narrator can mime the silent whistle signal for comic effect by blowing aimlessly and pulling faces. * "__________."]*

Norm let out the silent whistle signal that all gnats use in times of trouble, which sounds like this, * "__________." And seconds later thousands of his buzzing buddies appeared out of nowhere.

Norm told his friends about his plan and the rescue team flew off in the blustery conditions and landed on the whole length of the scythe handle. Their job was to flap their wings and hold the scythe in place so that it didn't fall and injure Riley.

Meanwhile, Loxly was still waiting to take action. The clouds got darker and thicker, and a second stronger gust of wind blew across the whole allotment. This caused the shed to shudder and the scythe inched forwards again slightly. Seconds later the sharp blade sliced right through the old and rusty nail and the scythe began to edge slowly towards Riley, who was still bending over the box of water melons.

Norm shouted to his friends, "Flap your little wings as hard as you can." And they flapped and flapped for all they were worth, but they couldn't hold on much longer. All went eerily quiet for a few moments then, WHOOSH! A huge final gust of wind blew in covering the whole allotment.

This was the last straw for the little gnats, they just couldn't hold on any longer. And with that the scythe began to fall quickly towards Riley, gathering speed as it fell. As the razor-sharp blade picked up speed it rattled and bounced down the side of Pullover's shed! Riley looked up and saw it coming towards him but, instead of moving out of the way he froze in panic.

This was when Loxly sprang into action. He ran as fast as he could towards Riley and when he'd picked up enough speed, he leapt high into the air and pushed him out of the way and into a clump of bushes, just in the nick of time. There was a final rattle and one last bounce, followed by a sickly squelching sound, as the scythe fell down on the top water melon in the box and it sliced in half!

Loxly remarked, "My, that was close." "You're not kidding," Norm added. Just then Frupp waddled over. "Hi there mate, having fun, are we?" He asked a stunned Riley. "What? Where? How?" Riley replied in shock. "Just a few more of my friends looking out for you," Frupp added. "Wow," Riley exclaimed, "I'd better say thank you to them."

"Sure, no problem," Frupp replied with a smile. "This is Loxly Fox, he lives here with his family and that's Norman the gnat and his friends. You'd better just thank him for saving you and he'll pass the message onto the other gnats, otherwise you'll be here all day!"

With a worried look on his face Riley said, "My mum's going to hit the roof when she finds out what's happened today!" "What you mean she's going to climb on top of your house," Frupp said with a confused look? Riley laughed his socks off and then put them back on again!

"Don't worry," Frupp said, "what happens on the allotment stays on the allotment." Riley didn't know what that meant, but he breathed a sigh of relief just the same.

"What I don't understand," Riley said, "is why grandad calls Pete, Pullover Pete?" Just then Furkitt hopped past on his way back to his pond and said, "Well his name is Pete, but he always wears a pullover no matter what the weather is like!" "And what about Bean Pole," Riley went on? "Oh, you mean Bean Pole Ben," Furkitt added? "It's quite simple, runner beans grow up a thin pole, and he's so slim that he has to lay down in the shower to get wet!"

Riley sighed, raised his eyebrows and with a smile said, "Yes well, that does sound like something grandad would say!" Riley said his goodbyes and also said he would see everyone tomorrow, then put the scythe back in Pullover Pete's shed.

Raking up trouble (Part 1)

It was the start of another hot day in Windowsill Ledge. The sun was out again and Riley was planning his fourth trip to grandad's allotment.

His dad was getting ready to start a new job and his mum had taken a week off from work to look after Riley. He asked his dad what his mum did at work and, with a smile on his face he replied, "Well son, as far as I know she just walks about all day talking to the customers that pop into her corner shop." "And what's the name of the shop Dad," Riley asked? "Harrods mate," he replied as he drove off!

With his dad out of the way, all Riley had to do now was see what his mum was up to, so he could make his way to the allotment with his bike, unnoticed. He'd dressed himself, put a drink, some sweets and his phone in a bag and was, as grandad would say, "Hot to trot."

Mum was on her phone to one of her best friends, Jennie. They were talking about make-up, handbags and what shops to visit next, so Riley knew she'd be busy for the next two hours at least!

Riley took his chance and tip-toed out of the kitchen door and into the hallway, where his bike was resting against the radiator. Then he passed by the front room door and made it out of his house and onto the street undetected – or so he thought!

Sitting in his car, a few doors down from Riley's house, was the stranger! He was busy writing notes on a clipboard, while hiding behind a newspaper. As Riley turned left at the top of his road the stranger started his big black car, so he could beat him to the allotment without being seen.

Five minutes later Riley arrived at grandad's shed. As he walked down the muddy path that ran up the middle of the allotment, and past one of the drippy taps, he heard a voice say quietly, but urgently, "Pssst, psssssssst."

It was Frupp and he was hiding behind a horse chestnut tree! Riley whispered back, "What, what's up?" And Frupp replied anxiously, "Quick hide, the stranger's about!" So, Riley dashed into the undergrowth behind Frupp to find out what was going on.

"He arrived here just after you left yesterday and was asking the shed owners about you," Frupp went on. "And he's turned up again this morning in his car!"

"Why is he so interested in me," Riley asked with a curious look on his face? "I'm not sure yet," Frupp replied, "but it's better to be safe than sorry, so you'd better keep your head down until we know more about him." "Mum and dad say you should never talk to strangers if you're by yourself," Riley added." "Hmmm, that's good advice," Frupp replied adding, "or get in their cars either."

Frupp and Riley watched as the stranger walked over and spoke to Wiff-Waff, another shed owner. And a few minutes later, they saw the stranger leaving the allotment, so the pair came out of hiding and began chatting about their friends.

"So," Riley said to Frupp, "how many friends have you got around here then?" "Well let's see," Frupp replied, "You've already met five of them so far, the rest you'll meet in the next few days I should think."

"What about your friends," Frupp asked Riley? "Let's see," he replied. "Well, my best friend is Sienna and she's my cousin too. Then there's my school friend's Millie, Joshua, Oscar and Luca as well."

Frupp said, "It sounds like we've got quite a lot of friends between us then." "Yes, I guess we have," Riley replied. "Right, I've got to shoot off for my lunch now," Frupp said urgently, "I'll catch up with you later."

"Oh, okay, Riley said, "what will you have?" "What I always have," Frupp replied, "half an hour with my feet in a puddle near the pond and then an hour in the sun." Frupp waddled slowly away and Riley was left on his own for a while.

He decided to ride around the allotment to see what was what and who was about, just to pass some time. Pullover Pete had turned up wearing his jumper, even though the sun was out, and Dust-pan Ann were there too. And Hardly-Ever had dropped in for a potter, but popped off pretty promptly, as usual!

Still on his own, and beginning to get a little bored now, Riley decided to do another lap of the allotment to see what everyone grew on their plots of land.

He was surprised when he saw just how many things could be grown in such small spaces. There were cabbages, rhubarb, runner beans, some beans that just stood still, and some people were growing tomatoes in green houses. They weren't green, but they were all made of glass!

Riley had nearly completed another lap of the allotment when he went passed a shed owned by a man that grandad called 'Rip Cord'. There he saw an old spikey tool that he hadn't seen before, leaning up against his water barrel.

It had a wooden handle, like the scythe he'd found, but it was dead straight, a little shorter and it seemed to be much lighter. Instead of a blade it had an odd-looking metal fitting, with a lot of short sharp spikes on it. And it was loosely held in place by a single rusty screw, which meant it wobble obble-obbled about all of the time.

Riley couldn't work out what it was, or how to use it at first, but that didn't stop him picking it up and fiddling about with it. By chance he looked up and, in the distance, he saw someone using the very same tool, and they were raking up dead leaves and twigs into neat piles. So, he decided that he would do the same outside Rip Cord's and grandad's shed to tidy them up, as he was still at a loose end.

It took him about 20 minutes, but when he'd finished everything looked shipshape and Bristol fashion, as grandad would say. As Riley didn't have a clue what that meant, he called it 'shedshaped and allotment fashion', as it made more sense!

His only mistake was forgetting to put the rake back from where he'd found it. Riley had left it on the ground, at front of the shed with the spikes pointing upwards!

Riley took off on his bike again to see what was happening in the pond. Furkitt was nowhere to be seen, but he did see some of his children working on their summer holiday projects, swimming around and practising their diving skills.

Just then the stranger pulled up in his car again. He got out, stood between two plots of land, and was now hiding behind a rusty corrugated iron barrier...

Raking up trouble (Part 2)

...Riley was running out of ideas of how to keep himself busy, so he thought he'd race to the end of the second muddy path that cuts roughly across the middle of the allotment and back again, and time himself. What he'd forgotten about, of course, was where he'd left the rickety rake!

Just as he'd pressed the stopwatch timer on his phone, the stranger slowly emerged again from behind the rusty corrugated iron barrier. And there was no doubt about it, he was definitely watching Riley for some reason! Fortunately, Burt the badger was slinking around, and from where he was standing it looked as if the stranger was going to jump out and grab Riley as he cycled past.

Burt said to himself, "Honesthssstly, you justhssst don't get the time to eat your breakfasthssst around here before thsssomething kickthsss off!" Just then Frupp waddled over and said to Burt quietly, "What's going on?" Burt whispered back, "The thssstranger's back on the prowl, what are we going to do?"

Frupp said in worried tone, "I can't do much to help, if the stranger spots me out in the open he'll know I can walk and talk and my secret will be out." "Yeah, me too," Burt agreed. "But hang on, I can move fasthster than you thso leave it to me, I've got thisss covered thson," Burt said reassuringly.

Frupp wasn't sure what he was going to do, but Burt had helped out in the past with emergencies such as this, and he was sure that he knew what he was doing. Meanwhile, Frupp hid amongst some bushes and watched as Burt sized up the problem in hand or the problem in paw in his case! Burt had seen Riley playing with the rickety rake earlier, and he'd also noticed where he'd left it.

By now Riley was shooting along so fast that he was leaving a dust trail behind him. He'd nearly reached Rip Cord's shed, and was close to the spot where he'd left the rickety rake. He was within seconds of bursting both of his tyres at the same time when Burt jumped out in front of him.

He stood up on his hind legs and began waving his front paws frantically. Then stuck his tongue out, shook his head from one side to the other a number of times and spluttered, "Blu-up-blu-up-blu-up-blu-up-blu-up-blu-up," really, really quickly.

Well, the odd noise alone was enough to make Riley slam on his brakes in shock! And after he did so, he shot over the handlebars of his bike, did a forward roll and landed back up on his feet, inches away from the sharp spikes of the rickety rake!

What he didn't know was that he was still in danger from the naughty spooky stranger. But it didn't matter because Burt was still on the case!

Riley said, "You must be another friend of Frupp's?" "Thsssure am, I'm Burt, are you okay," he asked? "Yeah, fine thanks, and thank you for saving me, dad would've gone nuts if he knew that he had to pay out for two new tyres." "Your dad turnthsss into nuthsss," Burt said, largely confused?

Riley chuckled to himself and said, "You're a funny lot down here, that's nothing," he added, "one day my mum laughed her head off!" "How on earth did she put it back on her neck," Burt asked, even more confused about this than the nut problem? "Ha, ha, ha, I'll tell you about that later," Riley said.

With that, he turned on his phone, put his earphones in, cued up his favourite CD and began to walk home with his bike, as his dad said it's dangerous to ride about if you can't hear what's going on around you.

Before picking his favourite track, Riley had bent down to wipe the mud and leaves off of his shoes and clothes before returning home, in case his mum saw the evidence of his outing. What he didn't know was that as he put his earphones in the stranger stepped out from behind the corrugated iron barrier again and was walking towards him really, really fast.

Burt saw what the stranger was up to, but didn't have time to warn Riley. So, before he ran for cover he moved forward quickly and covered up the nasty spikey parts of the rake with dead leaves.

It looked as if the stranger was just about to put both of his hands on Riley's shoulders when he stood on the spikey end of the rake! Well, the handle lifted up off of the ground at a terrific speed and the end of it spanked the stranger right on the end of his schnoze!

[Narrator can point to their nose].

The stranger was in a great deal of pain now. He rocked and reeled and hopped about in agony for a while and eventually spun around in a full circle. Still holding onto his nose, he fell backwards and disappeared from view into a huge rhubarb patch shouting, "OW, OW," and "OW," once more. A little later, still aching and ow-ing, the stranger sloped off back to his car unnoticed.

Riley was unsure what had happened, except he that saw some leaves fluttering back down to the ground. He pulled out his earplugs and said to Burt, "What was that?" "Oh nothsssing," Burt replied, looking happy with himself. "Juthssst the crowthsss in the nexthssst field having a party I should thsink."

"Okay, right, I really am off home this time before my mum spots that I'm missing and goes bananas," Riley said. "What," said Burt looking really confused again? "Your mum turnthsss into fruit?" Riley laughed out loud and said, "I'll tell you about it that next time I'm here.

"Ooh, but before I go," Riley added, "do you know why grandad call's that man Rip Cord?" "Oh he usethsssed to work at a parachute factory and wasthsss given a huge pay risethsss after only two daysthsss. Thssome thsssay a friend of his pulled a few thssstringsss for him," Burt said giggling to himself. "Very funny," Riley said!

"So, what about Wiff-Waff then," Riley asked expecting another daft answer? "Well," Burt said giggling. "All he ever thssseems to eat is beanthsss, and you know what they do to you don't you?" "Oh, right yes," Riley said laughing.

“Yes,” Burt said, “beanthsss, beanthsss, good for your heart, the more you eat the more you...” “THANK YOU, BURT,” Petunia butted in loudly, as she flew back to her nest. “That’s quite enough of that!”

After leaning the rake back up against Rip Cord’s water barrel, Riley said his goodbyes and left the allotment, smiling all the way home. What didn’t realise was that the next day things would get hotter than they ever had before!

F-F-F Fire! (Part 1)

It was a totally blue-sky day and without a doubt the hottest of Riley's summer holiday to date. And on this breeze-free morning everyone that braved the scorching heat seemed to be walking around in slow motion.

Even the animals on the allotment stayed in the shade, as they were saving up all of their energy until the sun had gone down to go and forage for food.

A broken bottle was the first thing that Riley saw as he pulled up outside Stationary Stan's shed on his bike, which is next door to grandad's shed. He found the shattered remains spread all over the place and being a thoughtful boy, he decided to clear it up before anyone or any animal cut themselves on it.

Riley borrowed Dust-pan Ann's dustpan to gather up the smaller pieces of jagged glass, then placed the whole lot, including the biggest piece, the base of the white bottle on top of Stan's compost heap, so at least people could see where it was.

Job done, he took off on his bike to see what was what and who was about. What he couldn't have known was that things were going to get even hotter a bit later on.

Prior to Riley's arrival, at around 11 o'clock, Furkitt had slipped deep inside the very same compost heap that Riley had placed the broken glass on.

There were clumps of brown tinder-dry grass on top, but lower down it was much, much cooler and nice and damp too. It was the perfect spot for an over-heated amphibian to take a mid-morning snooze.

At midday the sun was at its highest and hottest point in the sky and its rays were beating down relentlessly on everything, but it would be the base of the broken bottle which would prove to be the source of a dangerous ignition.

As the sun reached just the right or wrong angle, as the case maybe, the base of the broken bottle began to magnify the sun's rays. And in no time at all it concentrated the heat of the sun into a single laser-like beam and the dried grass under the bottle began to smoulder and smoke a little.

The timing of the 12:03 express train through the towns over ground station could not have been worse. One hundred and eighty tons of metal and woodwork shot through at a little over 120mph, and the knock-on effect caused a silent after-shock in the shape of a wide and spiralling volume of wind.

The enormous gust rose up and over the station's grassy embankment, covering the whole length of it like an enormous invisible moving duvet towards the line of fir trees by the pond. The path of the wind then funnelled its way between the trunks of the trees and over the edge of the allotment, eventually fanning the already smoking compost heap, and WHOOSH - up it went in flames!

Meanwhile, Furkitt was still snoozing and snoring away, totally unaware he was now in serious danger. Luckily for him a bunch of rose stems that were above him began to split and crackle in the intense heat and he woke up coughing and spluttering.

His first words were, "Oi-oi, braaap, flipping braaap-braaap." Which as you know means know means, "'elp flipping 'elp, flipping 'elp, 'elp," in frog language! And he shot out of a hole in the side of the burning heap.

"Ooh my good Gawd," Petunia shrieked, as she flew overhead, "It'll all end in tears, better get some water on that before the flames reach another shed," she added frantically. Minutes later the flames were over eight feet high and the smoke was marking out the path of the sprawling wind.

The intensity of the circular backdraft from the train began bending the flames towards the left-hand end of Stan's shed. Things were turning from bad to worse all too quickly and it was only going to get, "Worser-err," as grandad would say!

You see, there was a paraffin-soaked rag hanging out of Stan's broken window and half of it was resting on a huge pile of bone-dry newspapers. The tip of the flickering fire just managed to lick the edges of the rag and POOF - up it went in flames!

The compost heap had almost burnt down now, but the shed and its contents were the next source of fuel for fire. In the middle of the shed, on a chair, was a large tin of varnish. And to the right of that, tucked away in a corner, was a gas stove cylinder - both of which were highly inflammable!

Riley rushed back to the scene when he saw the huge plumes of black and grey smoke billowing over the allotment and bumped into Furkitt, who was still coughing and spluttering. Riley said with a great deal of urgency, "What are we going to do Furkitt, this is really serious?"

"The first thing to do," Furkitt said, "is...PANIC!" And they both stared into each other's eyes and screamed, "WAAAAAAAARGH," for exactly two seconds! "Right," Furkitt went on, "now that's out of the way follow me, I know who can help us."

Riley followed Furkitt to a shed that he'd hadn't noticed before, which was tucked away at the top of the allotment. And there behind it, close to the line of fir trees, were five hives, full of sleeping honey bees.

“Gosh,” said Riley in surprise, “I didn’t know that these were here.” “Well,” Furkitt said, “we keep it on a nudge-nudge, wink-wink basis on the allotment, as your grandad would say, because the bees need to be left alone to get on with their work without being disturbed.” “Oh, I see,” Riley said.

Furkitt hopped over to the first hive and Riley was close behind him. Barry the bee was on guard duty that morning and he said to Furkitt. “Eye-eye, I think you’ll be needing need our help, won’t you?” Furkitt replied with a wheeze, “We sure could.” “Okay,” Barry said buzzily, “I’ll wake the troops.” And with that he passed the word onto the other four hives, and pretty soon the whole allotment was alive with bees.

“What’s occurring,” said one bee to another? “Looks like we’re on fire duty again Blossom.” “Lummy,” replied Bernadette, “We’d better get organised then.”

Just then a message came through from big Bertha, the Queen bee of hive one. It read, “You all know what to do my brave and loyal subjects, so do your duty and save our allotment, while I have a right Royal lay down and breakfast in bed!”

The bees immediately began to form ranks, with a 100 bees per rank. Then, at great speed, they flew towards the pond. Once there they swooped down onto the surface of the water, one rank after another, each picking up a single droplet of water with their hind legs.

Riley noticed what they were doing and said to Furkitt, “I can’t see how this is going to put the fire out.” “Just wait mate, we’ve done this before,” Furkitt said confidently. And minutes later there were 170,000 bees all of whom were now carrying a miniature water bomb each.

Amongst the first wave of bees were Basil and his brother Bond, along with Bob, Bart, Betty and Bonnie and her adopted brother, Clyde. And they were closely followed by Bill, Blossom, Bernadette and Algernon Pilkington Smith-Smythe-Smith, who was on holiday from a hive in Oxford. He wasn’t happy with the situation by any stretch of the imagination and muttered to himself, “I didn’t sign up for this,” but he joined in any way!

Stan’s shed was fully alight at the left-hand end now, and the fire was creeping ever closer to the tin of varnish and the very naughty explosive gas cylinder!

In a flash of inspiration Riley had a brain wave, which isn't surprising. Most of the Walton's are known for their wavy brains! He ran and picked up a hosepipe and attached it to the nearest drippy tap, but it wasn't long enough to reach the shed.

Undeterred by this set back he found a bucket near Stan's shed and went over to his water barrel and filled it up. Then he ran back and threw it over the fire. After the hissing and had died down Furkitt said, "Nice touch son, keep it up, every little drop helps as you're about to see."

The bees had split up into two large swarms now, one half to the left of the burning shed and the other to the right of it. Then, at rate of knots well, 15 to 20mph that is, the two sections flew directly towards each other over fire!

Riley couldn't work out what they were doing and muttered in dismay, "Oooh, this isn't going to end well." Just than Burt the badger slinked by and said reassuringly, "I've thsseen it all before thssson, justhssst thsssit and watch nature working at its besthssst..."

F-F-F Fire! (Part 2)

...At the very last second, just before the bees would've collided into each other, they pulled up sharply and flew straight up in the air like a huge squadron of miniature fighter planes at an air display. As they did so the droplets of water dislodge from their hind legs due to the speed that they were travelling at. Tiny droplets of water smashed into thousands of other tiny droplets. And as they joined up and fell, they became much larger drops of water! This continued until the bees had created a concentrated rain shower, which then dropped directly on top of Stan's shed. This didn't put the fire out, but it did dampen it down, and gave the bees' time to go back to the pond for a refill.

"I'm Impressed," Riley said, with a bit more hope in his heart! "Cool eh," Furkitt said, adjusting his hat. As the bees topped up with water for a second time a muffled phut was heard. This was the lid of the varnish tin popping off due to the heat and the sticky content was now burning furiously.

The bees repeated their dive-bombing exercise, but even they could see they were up against it. Riley said with some urgency, "Were going to have to call the Fire Brigade you know Furkitt!" "Great idea," he said enthusiastically. "Have you got your magic talking box with you," he asked hopefully? "I sure have," Riley replied with a grin, and he reached inside his bag and pulled out his mobile phone.

"OH NO," he said loudly, "the battery's dead!" "DEAD," Furkitt said in horror! "We haven't got time to arrange a funeral now you know, we've got to deal with the fire first!" "No, you twit," Riley replied sharply, "it needs charging up."

"Well, that's a fat lot of good that is," Norman the gnat said as he circled over the pair. "What about the old phone box," he added with a smile? "Brilliant idea," said Furkitt! And they both led Riley to a tarnished old red telephone box, which was tucked away behind a large gorse bush not far from Stan's shed.

“Oh my gosh,” Riley said, a little taken aback, “what the heck is that?” “Well, it’s not Dr Who’s Tardis, but it is a box for making phone calls apparently,” Norm said totally in charge for once. Riley said apologetically, “But… but… I don’t know how it works,” is it connected to the internet,” he added? “The inter-what-where-net,” Norm said largely confused again?

“Look,” said Furkitt, “the instruction are on the inside.” And the sign on the phone said, insert coins and push button A to be heard. And, push button B to get your change back. “Hang on a minute,” Riley said hastily, “it only works with old money, not with this new decimal toot, as grandad would say.”

“Need a hand old boy,” Loxly said as he ambled by? “Oh, I see your problem,” he added, “step aside, I’ve done this before matey-boy.” And Loxly entered the phone box brimming with confidence.

He hit the coin collection tray once on the left-hand side, twice on the right-hand side and once underneath it with his paw and WALLOP, the coin tray door sprang open to reveal 27 uncollected old pennies. “Top work Loxly,” said Norm smiling, “now let’s get to work.”

Riley picked up the old handset and was stunned to hear that it still had a dialling tone! He followed the instructions on the phone to the letter and then dialled 999.

“Which service do you require caller, police, ambulance or the fire service,” a calm voice said? A now calmer Riley replied, “The fire service please.” He gave the lady all of the details that she asked for and then she informed him that a fire engine would be on its way immediately. Then he, Furkitt, Norm, Petunia and Loxly all returned to the burning shed to see how the bees were getting on.

They had just finished their fifth bombing raid when Bartholomew, the number one bee from the first hive, noticed that the pond level was dropping considerably. The fire was just under control, but it was still burning, so he announced his plan B to the whole swarm.

“Okay,” he said loudly, “listen up, we’re going to have to split up and use what’s in the water barrels.” And in seconds the bees separated into smaller groups and began skimming the surface of every barrel on the allotment.

By now the fire had spread to over half of Stan's shed and the naughty gas cylinder was next on its menu. Without warning, there was an enormous BANG!

The explosion blew out the walls and windows of the flimsily made shed at the same time! And the roof shot into the air and came down with a crunch, smothering some of the flames as it did so! Furkitt's hat was blown clean off and everyone present got a good coating of smoke and ash.

"Wow that was close," Riley said, as the fire engine arrived. Safe in the knowledge that all was nearly under control, the bees returned to their hives and Furkitt, Norm, Petunia and Loxly all slipped away unnoticed.

After the firemen had made sure that the blaze was out, and had soaked it with gallons of water just to make sure, the fire chief went over to chat with Riley.

You did the right thing calling us young man, most people would've tried to put out a fire like this by themselves. "However," the fire chief added, "I couldn't help notice that the ground around the whole shed was damp before we arrived, you err, you didn't have any help from anyone did you," he asked questioningly?

"No," Riley said quietly, looking down and kicking at the ground with one foot. "No err, no help from the bees at all then," the chief went on? "WHAT?" "NO," Riley said far too loudly and even less convincingly!

"Hmmm," the fire chief muttered, as he bent down and looked Riley squarely in the eyes. "I used to come here with my grandad." He spoke. "Oh... right," Riley said nervously. "Oh yes," the chief carried on, "met some really nice people down here and got to know the wild life that lives around here too."

"R-e-a-l-l-y," Riley said, even more nervously than before. "Hmmm yes," the chief said. "Let's see, there was a frog, a pigeon, a gnat, a badger, a magpie and even a fox if I remember rightly, ooh and there were a couple of squirrels too I believe."

The fire chief was clearly remembering all of the good times that he'd spent at the allotment, but Riley was thinking, "Oh this guy just won't shut up, he'll say something else soon I bet!"

"Mind you," the chief went on as expected, "that was a long time ago, their children would've taken over by now I would've thought; I wonder where they all are now?" Shrugging his shoulders and itching to get away Riley said, "I dunno... I'm only seven. I mean, it's not as if it's the Hundred Acre Wood around here is it, it's just an allotment isn't?"

Riley gulped more than once and thought, "He knows, he knows all about this place, what am I going to say if he asks me about what goes on around here?"

Fortunately, at this point, the fire chief stood up and began walking towards his crew and the fire engine saying, "I'm off now then, please say hi to Mr and Mrs Twizzy for me, will you?" Riley was more than relieved, so much so that he dropped his guard and said loudly, "OKAY, WILL DO."

Realising his school boy error, he said to himself, "Oh suuuuuuurely not!" The fire chief didn't look back, he just kept on walking, waved his left hand in the air and then drove off back to the fire station.

Just then Frupp waddled over and Loxly was just behind him. Frupp said cheerfully, "Well you've had an eventful day then, you've met the bees and put a fire out too!" Riley said shyly, "Well, I couldn't have done it without some help that's for sure."

And with that Riley said, "I'm off home now, see you tomorrow Loxly?" "Yes, see you tomorrow old bean. I might be a tad late I'm on the prowl tonight, got to get the cubs their breakfast you know."

As Riley left and pulled out into Karmasulike Crescent he thought to himself, "Hmmm, I haven't seen the stranger in a while, that can only be a good thing - right?"

Loxly's late (Part 1)

It was the weekend, the hardest time for Riley to slip out of the house, as both of his parents were at home. Luckily on this Saturday morning his dad was working on the inside of his new 'man cave', his very own garden shed, and his mum was busy looking for a new handbag online, as she only had twenty-nine old ones! The weather had taken a turn for the worst overnight and the day began with a dark and cloudy sky. As Riley peered through his bedroom window, he was thinking twice about visiting the allotment, as the rain was now beginning to puddle it down.

He changed his mind immediately however, as during his breakfast he heard a disturbing news flash on the television. The gloomy start to the morning would go onto set the tone for the rest of the day.

"Good morning," the presenter said, "I'm Drew Nicely and here is your local news, and this is our top story."

"Animal rights campaigners are protesting outside of The Windowsill Ledge Hunt Lodge today, as it seems yet another fox has been killed."

Riley couldn't believe what he was hearing, and he was so shocked that he sprayed the mouthful of cereal he was eating all over the coffee table in front of him! As the story unfolded, he realised that he might have to cope with the fact that his new friend Loxly, was dead!

"No evidence of the animal has been found at the scene yet," the newscaster went on, "however, a hunt protester's young son found a small bright yellow, but blood-stained waistcoat, in the lower meadow of the farmer's land. Let's go over live to our reporter out in the field, Sonia Shoulder. What's happening Sonia?"

At the mention of a yellow waistcoat Riley's heart sank and he froze in his chair as he listened to the rest of the news report.

"Hi Drew," the reporter replied, "well it's a bit of a mystery, but what we do know is that at 8 a.m. this morning the hunt began and the hunt master, Major Eyes-Water said that they were drag hunting as usual. This means that a scent trail is laid for the hounds to follow instead of hunting for foxes. But it seems that a fox may have been caught and killed by the hounds as it crossed the trail while it foraged for food."

"Curiously Drew," the reporter added, "no one knows where the waistcoat has come from. "Stranger still, it's far too small for an adult and more even more curiously, it wouldn't fit a small child either!"

Riley wanted to turn off the television and pretend it wasn't happening, but he couldn't move. A few seconds later he heard the news reporter say, "Anyway Drew, this is what Major Eyes-Water had to say earlier."

"Well, it's just one of things isn't it, we were drag hunting as we always do," he said lying through his teeth, "when I noticed the hounds in the corner of the lower meadow." "All sixty hounds," the reporter said pointedly! "And do you think that it's fair to hunt one animal with such a large pack," the reporter asked with a frown?

"Well, it's a bit of sport isn't it, and we do protect the environment too don't forget." "Also," the pompous and over-weight Major went on, "if you're tied to a desk for nine hours a week it's nice to let the clutch out at the weekend in the countryside don't you think?"

The Major was standing next to his equally pompous and stick-thin wife during the interview, and she chomping at the bit to add her tuppence worth on the situation. "Well," she said in a huff. "I don't know what all the fuss is about, it's not our fault if a silly little fox crosses our path is it? I mean really, they are vermin after all!"

Riley's blood began to boil and his little heart was banging against his rib cage and he became angrier and angrier. So angry in fact that he dropped his cereal bowl on the floor and broke into a string of butcher's back slang that grandad had taught him, so that he could let off steam without sounding rude.

Riley growled under his breath, "Just look at 'em, and look at that di-puts namow (stupid woman) with him, I'd like to k-naps (spank) her backside with the rough end of a toilet brush!"

"What a pair of idiots," he said out loud! Then he stood up in a rage and stomped around the front room shouting, "NO, NO, NO, NO you di-puts d-lo pollods," (stupid old dollops) as tears streamed down his little e-caf (face). Still fuming at the news, he went on, "Really, they've got all that yenom, (money) but all that they can think of to do is chase a little fox around and then kill it - really brave!"

Wiping the tears from his face Riley grabbed his bag and bike and stormed out of the house in a great big steaming hurry, slamming the front door behind him.

As the crashing noise of the front door slamming echoed around the house Riley's mum walked into the front room to see what was going on. "Oh my God," she said in alarm! "Look at the mess in here," adding, "right, that's it, that boy has been acting strangely all week, tonight we're going to have a serious mum and dad talk and get to the bottom of this!"

As Riley entered the allotment off of Karmasulike Crescent he opened the three-bar gate and the first person that he ran into was the stranger!

"RIGHT," he said in a fierce temper, "THAT'S IT, I don't know who you are or what you want and I really don't care anymore, but if you don't push off right now, I'll get my dad or call the police, it's up to you pal!"

The stranger was so startled by Riley's outburst that he dropped his clipboard. Then he tripped over his own feet and fell headfirst straight into a drainage ditch and wasn't seen for the rest of the day.

The rain began to ease up as Riley approached Loxly's den, which was tucked away under the planking at the back of Ron Seal's shed. There was an eerie and unnatural silence over the whole allotment that sad morning. Every animal on the allotment stood stock-still - and the birds had stopped singing too.

As the last few drips and drops of rain fell from the outstretched branches and the leaves of the trees in Twizzy Wood, it sounded as if they were all crying at the loss of their old friend.

With his head slightly bowed and tears about to surface again, Riley made a slow and deliberate walk to tell Loxly's wife, Layla the terrible news.

She was pacing up and down outside of the den with a concerned look on her face, as she kept a motherly eye on her four playful cubs. "Hallo Riley," she said quietly, "I'm worried about Loxly. He went out last night, but he hasn't come home yet."

“I… I know,” Riley said slowly, beginning to well up. “I’m afraid he’s… he’s not coming back, he’s… he’s been…,” “Killed by the hunt hounds,” Layla said, finishing off his painful sentence. “Yes, I think so,” Riley replied. And with that he burst into a flood of tears that he could not stop. Shaking his head he said, “I’m so, so sorry, I don’t know what to do or say and worst of all I can’t fix this, I feel awful.”

As he sobbed his little heart out Layla cradled Riley in her paws as the bad news began to sink in. She didn’t cry, she held her head up high and eventually said, “Right, first thing first, I’ve got cubs to feed.”

“You’re being very brave Layla,” Riley said, sniffing and wiping his cheeks with his trembling hands. “Well,” she said, “this is how things are in the wild, it’s not fair, but we must carry on. That’s what Loxly would’ve done and that’s what I will do…”

Loxly's late (Part 2)

...Straight away Riley, Frupp and Furkitt all said together, "We'll stay with the cubs," but there was no need for cub-sitting. At that very moment Ronnie and Reggie, the grey squirrels arrived on the scene. They had heard the news that one of their oldest friends had been killed by hunt hounds, and they weren't happy about it at all.

"Who are they," Riley asked quietly? "Oh," Frupp said, "that's the twins, they look after all of the animal's interest on the allotment and make sure that they're all safe, you might say!"

Ron said, "We've just 'eard about Loxly and it displeases us greatly, dunnit Reg? "It does Ron, it does," Reg replied. "We thought you might need this," Ron said to Layla, and he gave her a heavy basket. When she looked inside, she found two plump chickens. "We-err, we 'found' 'em on our rounds," Reg said with a grin. Layla thanked them and gave them a hug each.

"Hallo," Ron said to Frupp in surprise, "who's this then," noticing Riley! "This is Riley, a new friend of ours, and although he only knew Loxly for a short time he's really angry and upset about what's happened."

"Yes, we all are, but we're 'ere to put things right." Ron said to Riley as he reached into his pocket, "'ere you go son, dry your eyes, blow your nose and smarten up your hair." And he gave him a handkerchief and a comb. "Thanks mate," Riley said.

"Thank you so much for the food boys, and say hallo to your mum for me," Layla said gratefully, "but what can we do about the hunt," she asked finally breaking down in tears herself?

Ron patted and held her left paw in his and said in a low and gruff voice, "You just leave that to me and Reg and if there's anything you need, anything at all," he added, "just ask." And with that Ron and Reg left the allotment to hatch a plan of revenge on the hunt.

Before Riley left the allotment, he said to Layla that he would bring her some more food on Sunday, and asked her what she needed? "Ooh," she said, "let me think - I know, some wriggly-iggly earthworms and some fruit would be lovely thank you."

Riley walked home in daze, heartbroken after the worst day of his little life. He ached all over and his eyes were sore from where he'd cried so much.

He was still upset when he got home and his mum could see that he'd been crying and said, "What on earth's wrong Riley?" "Oh, nothing really," he replied with a quiet sigh, and then he slipped off upstairs to his room.

A little later his mum went up to see how he was and to tell him that his tea was ready, but he wasn't very hungry. "Come on," she said, "tell me what's wrong," she asked him again holding his hand. "Well," he said slowly looking up from his pillow, "it's my friend Loxly, he... he was killed today." "WHAT," his mum said in shock? "That's terrible news!" Then she thought, "Hang on a minute, he doesn't know anyone called Loxly?"

When Jack, Riley's dad came home from work his mum said to him in tears, "I think we're going to have to take Riley to the doctors." "What on earth for," he asked with a worried look on his face? "He was talking double Dutch this morning and when he came in earlier, he said that his friend, Loxly had been killed! The thing is," she added, "we don't know anyone called Loxly, do you think he's got an imaginary friend," she asked blowing her nose?

"Could be," his dad said, "lots of children do and I'm sure it's nothing to worry about." He put his arm around her shoulders and said, "Don't worry, I'm seeing Dr Stetic to night. "Oh, you mean Anna," Riley's mum asked? "Yes that's right," Riley's dad replied. "The riding club have organised a bike ride over the cycle dips in the forest, I'll see what she has to say."

Later that evening, Ron and Reg slipped into the farmer's house through a hole his thatched roof. And there, sitting at a long oak table in his kitchen were Major Eyes-Water and the farmer. They were talking about the Sunday hunt and Ron and Reg didn't like what they heard at all.

"Don't worry," the Major said smugly, "we'll do what we always do, we'll take the dragging gear with us so it looks as if we're obeying the law, but still bag a fox or two so that your chickens will be safe. Do you err, do you have the necessary cashy-wonga to ensure that we'll use your fields next year," he asked pressingly?" The farmer nervously fiddled with his cap a number of times and then sheepishly handed the Major a brown envelope with £2000 inside it! "Capital," the Major said, "capital."

"Oh dear, oh dear Reg," Ron said glumly, "it appears that we 'ave a bit of jiggery-pokery late-night-snookery occurrin' on our patch." "Oh dear, oh dear Ron," Reg replied just as glumly. "It looks as if mum was right you know," Reg added, "There's no e-koms (smoke) without e-rif." (fire)

"This is most disappointing," Ron went on. "Tutty-tut-tut," Reg replied with a disapproving look. "Someone should put a stop to it," Reg added. "Back to the office is it Ron," he asked? "I believe so Reg, I believe so." Ron replied.

The artful twins strolled out of the farmer's roof at a leisurely pace and made tracks back to their drey in the fir tree opposite the old telephone box, where they would hatch a plan to stop the Sunday hunt.

As the night closed in Riley was tucked up in bed, while his mum waited nervously for his dad to return to hear what their doctor had to say about him.

When she heard a key turn in the lock she dashed to the front door and said hurriedly, "Well, well, what did the doctor say?" Riley's dad smiled and replied, "It's like I said, there's nothing to worry about." "But... but," Riley's mum went on, "why has he suddenly got an imaginary friend, I don't understand?" "Let me get in and I'll tell you what she said," Riley's dad said.

A few minutes later Riley's dad sat down with a cup of tea in front of the fire and said, "Firstly, there's no need to worry. Riley is still a youngster and his brain is still growing. This means that his imagination is growing as well, and it's a healthy sign that he's creating thoughts in his mind."

"Secondly," he added, "if you think about it, we're always telling him what to do, so if he has an imaginary friend around, he can tell them what to do. And to put your mind at rest, rather than see Riley at the surgery, the doctor thought it would be better to meet up with us all tomorrow at the allotment."

And with that Riley's mum and dad headed off to bed, hoping that tomorrow would be a much better day.

A Major upset (Part 1)

Sunday arrived. However, it arrived much earlier for Riley. He had set him alarm for half past five in the morning, and his plan was to take the food that he'd promised Layla and return home before his mum and dad realised that he was up. He crept down stairs and out into the back garden and began digging for worms. He wasn't having much luck though. The ground was so hard and dry that his spade wouldn't cut through the sun-baked earth.

A little voice said, "You need some rain, worms always pop up when it's raining." Riley looked up to see Petunia sitting on his fence. He whispered, "Oh hi

Petunia, well it doesn't look like it's going to rain at the moment, what am I going to do?"

"Way ahead of you," she said with a grin, "park yourself on the garden bench, you're going to enjoy this." After a swift aerial display a flock of starlings landed and covered most of the lawn. "Right girls," Petunia said, "now do your stuff," and then she went and sat down beside Riley.

For two minutes on the trot the starlings ran around all over the grass, then they suddenly stopped dead in their tracks with their heads tilted to one side. "What's going on, what are they doing," Riley asked with a confused look? "They're pretending to be rain," she replied, "and now they're listening for the worms. Their feet copy the sound of rain falling and then up come the worms, cute eh!" "I'll say," Riley replied with a broad smile.

Five minutes later the whole garden was crawling with wriggly-iggly earthworms. The starlings took one each for themselves and put the rest in Riley's bucket, which was now full to the brim.

"Wow," said Riley, "I'm impressed, thanks for your help, I must get on now." He grabbed four apples and bananas from the fruit bowl in the kitchen, hooked his bucket over the handle bars of his bike and made his way to the allotment.

Riley approached Layla's den as quietly as he could, because he didn't want to wake her or the cubs up. He peered inside and could see her tail swishing and twitching, and her cubs were still fast asleep. So he pushed the food in next to her, so that when she woke up breakfast would be ready and waiting for them. He was just about to get on his bike when he heard laughter coming from behind Ron and Reg's fir tree.

"Oh yes," he said quietly, peering around the tree trunk, "and what are you two giggling about at this time of the day?" "Oooh, hallo son," Ron said. "Well," Reg said with a smirk, "a naughty occurrence has occurred in the small hours of Saturday and looks as if the Sunday hunt will have to be cancelled after all.

Ron, Reg and the rest of the squirrels of Twizzy Wood spent their time collecting all of the conkers that they could find. Then they peeled off the skins, mashed them up and put the mixture into their back packs, ready for their visit to the hunt hound's pen. When they arrived, they put a small helping in each of the hound's food bowls, knowing that the conkers would upset their stomachs.

"Oh," Riley said! "Will it harm them," he asked? "No," said Reg confidently, "but they won't feel like dancing about that's for sure." "Oh no," Reg added, "they won't have the strength to bark, let alone chase anything today."

Riley headed for home at this point and couldn't wait to get back under his duvet. He was tired, but happy that something had been done to stop the hunt.

At 8 o'clock sharp the Major and his wife were sitting on their horses, trying to get the hunt underway. "TANTIVY, YOICKS AWAY KENNELMAN," the Major bellowed. "What," said the kennelman, helping himself to another drink from a stirrup cup? "Let the hounds out you buffoon," the Major whispered. "Oh right, hic," the tipsy kennelman replied, stumbling towards the hound's pen.

He rattled the keys in the lock and was surprised when he was met with a deathly hush! The kennelman undid the gate and went in, where he noticed that the hound's food bowls had been licked clean.

Then he waddled over to where they slept only to find dogs strewn all over the place, but none were standing up! Most were still asleep, some were groaning and holding their stomachs and a few others were still being sick.

In a huff the Major's wife said, "Hey you there, what's wrong you silly little man?" Gritting his teeth, the kennelman replied, "It's the dogs mam, thems is ill," followed under his breath with, "you great big dozy dollop." "WHAT," the Major shouted, "impossible, I fed 'em myself bright and early and they were in fine fettle!"

"You'd better come see for yourself sir," the kennelman remarked, "thems is definitely ill alright." And the Major pushed past him and strode into the hound's pen wondering what on earth the problem could be. "See sir," the kennelman said, "it's like I said, sick as pigs them are."

"What am I going to do," the Major said, worrying more about the money that he'd spent on the hunt than his hounds? "Dash and blast," he blustered, "I'll have to hand back all of that lovely cashy-wonga to the riff raff that wanted to join the hunt."

Back at home Riley's dad was about to wake him up. "Come on son," he said, "up you get, we've got to go to the allotment and I've got check grandad's shed roof for leaks." "Hmmm," Riley murmured rubbing his eyes as his dad opened his curtains.

A few seconds later Riley woke up with a start! He thought he'd overslept and hadn't taken Layla's food to her. When he realised that he'd already dropped it off he sank back into his pillows for a few more minutes. Then he thought, "Hang on a minute, dads got a key to grandad's shed, how come I didn't know that?" Then he said out loud in a disgruntled fashion, "It's because I'm only seven isn't it!"

Riley got washed and dressed and had breakfast with his mum and dad. As a treat, and as she knew their doctor would see him today, his mum made him a snack box so that he could stay at the allotment all day.

At 9:30 a.m. they all set off to the allotment, and as they passed the hunt stables Riley started giggling. There he saw a red-faced Major who was still trying to work out what had happened to his hounds, while his wife walked around in a fluster trying to explain to the other riders why the hunt had to be cancelled.

"Look," Riley's dad said as he began unlocking grandad's shed, "it's 'Pardon' the doctor's assistant." "Come on then," Riley said expecting a daft answer, "why do you and grandad call her Pardon?" "Well," Riley's dad said beginning to laugh, "her real name is Miss Heard and she's a little deaf in one ear!" "Oh my gosh," Riley said raising his eyebrows, "and mum thinks that there's something wrong with me!"

Just then Anna Stetic, the doctor arrived on her bicycle, and after saying hallo to everyone she asked Riley if he would show her around the allotment.

After a few minutes she said, "I can see why people come here, it's just so peaceful." "So," she went on, "your mum's a bit worried and she wanted me to have a chat with you just as a check-up, if that's okay?"

Just then a twig fell out of nowhere and hit Riley on his back. When he looked around, he saw two beady eyes blinking at him from the undergrowth. It was Frupp and he was slowly waving a branch and mouthing the words, "Don't say anything about this place or our secret is out." When the doctor looked down and glanced into the pond for a few seconds Riley mouthed back, "Don't worry I won't."

As the doctor looked back up and turned to faced Riley again, he said, “I’m fine, as far as I know, I don’t know what all the fuss is about. I’ve got an invisible friend, loads of children do, don’t they,” he asked with a frown?

“Yes but…,” the doctor said trying to make a point. But Riley cut her short with, “I mean, there are people here that talk to their plants and you don’t see them speaking to a doctor do you!” And he walked off in a huff. Realising that she couldn’t argue with his reasoning she walked over to speak to Riley’s mum…

A Major upset (Part 2)

... "Well Mrs Walton, you'd better sit down," the doctor said. "Why, what on earth's wrong, is it something serious," Riley's mum asked? "It's as I feared, Riley has a severe case of 'allotmentitus'," the doctor said with huge grin. "It's nothing to worry about really," she went on. "Most children have an imaginary friend at some point in their lives but, in time, the friends just fade away as quickly as they arrive."

Meanwhile, Riley watched as his dad locked up grandad's shed and gave the windows a wipe over with a damp cloth. His mum and dad left him there at the allotment with his elevenses box and said they would see him later at home for his evening meal.

With still so many people around Riley knew that the gang would be hiding somewhere in the shadows of the allotment. So, he mounted his bike, circled around and tried to find them.

He'd just pulled up short of Stationary Stan's shed when he saw Frupp lurking at the back of the gorse bush, near the old telephone box. Making sure that he wasn't being followed or watched, Riley pushed his way in towards him.

As he got close enough to whisper to Frupp, Petunia landed on his head breathless and panting. "Stranger," she said trying to catch her breath, "the strangely stranger's back, and this time he's got a radio!"

"Right," Frupp said with a stern glare, "that does it, it's high time we dealt with him once and for all!" "Norm," he barked, "go and wake the bees up!" "Ron - Reg," he said sharply, "have you still got a stash of spare acorns," he asked? "Would a sack full be enough," Ron asked? "Yes," said Frupp, "that'll do nicely."

Then he said to Furkitt, "Can you hop off and find Burt the badger?" "Will do," Furkitt replied straightening his cap. "Anything I can do," Max the magpie said as he flew past? "Yes," Riley said, "can you rouse the squadron?" "Will do, Roger that," Max said with delight. "Right," Frupp said finally, "meet me back here in 10 minutes."

And with that the gang set off to carry out the first part of Frupp's plan. Meanwhile, Frupp slowly edged his way over to the pond to ponder over his plan, and to get a much-needed drink of water.

Refreshed and thinking more clearly, he sidled his way back to the old telephone box, where he found his friends all present and correct and ready to go. "Right," he said quietly, "here's what we're going to do," and then he began to whisper his plan into the waiting ears of his friends.

" We'll wait until midday, because that's when the shed owners have a break for lunch, and there will be less people about. Then we'll psss-ssswersss ssswersss-ssswersss, and ssswersss ssswersss ssswersss ssswersss," he whispered on.

"And finally, we'll psss-ssswersss and psss-ssswersss then psss-ssswersss his ssswersss-ssswersss - got it," Frupp asked? And the whole gang said together, "psss ssswersss," which in whispering language means, "okey-dokey."

Still with 40 minutes to wait before 'Operation Stranger' could get underway, the gang separated so they could organise themselves for the tasks in hand. Max, Petunia, Norm and the bees and Ron and Reg would be in charge of the air space over the stranger, while Frupp, Burt and Riley would take care of things on the ground - Riley being the bait for the trap.

As Frupp blended back into the shadows Riley moved out into the open to see if he could find out where the stranger was and what he was up to. It didn't take long to spot him; he was sitting under a tree with a wide trunk near the entrance of the allotment. Riley sat down behind a greenhouse a few feet away to keep an eye on the stranger movements, and kept himself busy by playing a game on his phone while he waited patiently for zero hour.

Between eating a sandwich and sipping at his tea, the stranger was speaking to someone on his radio. And Riley heard him say, "Suspect located HQ, will follow on foot and report back after my break."

At last the church bell struck 12 o'clock. And while the stranger was busy reading his newspaper Riley crept his way around to the back of the tree he was sitting under. Then, using his elbows, he crawled quietly forwards on his stomach so that he was near the stranger's feet. Once he was in position, he carefully undid each of his boot laces and then tied them both together in tight knots.

Then, bold as brass, Riley stepped right out in front of the stranger and grinned at him. He then leant forward and ripped his newspaper in half, from top to bottom! The stranger looked up with a fierce stare and said in surprise, "Oi - what do you think you're doing?"

Riley didn't answer him straight away, he just inhaled as much air into his lungs as possible. Then he blew a long and loud raspberry at him and said, "Bet you can't catch me sucker!"

Well, the stranger was furious. He stood up and began to chase Riley but, it was only then that he realised that there was something wrong with his feet. He dropped his sandwich first, then knocked over his flask of tea and finally fell flat on his face. By this time Riley had shot off up the muddy path, laughing all the way, towards the second drippy tap at the top of the allotment.

Eventually realising that it was his laces that were the cause of the problem, he tried frantically to undo them. But, as they were tied in such small knots, and he had such large fingers, it was impossible. In a rage he pulled his boots off and began running after Riley in just his socks. This would prove to be a fatal error a little later on.

Fully believing that he was now trouble-free, a determined glare coupled with a smirk returned to the stranger's face as he chased after Riley. The stranger was in arms reach of him now, and he was just about to grab him with both of his hands when Frupp sent a signal to Petunia, Max and the magpie squadron, who were circling above. He raised then dropped his right branch and the birds released a length of netting right over the stranger's head.

Riley, who was ahead of him again, turned to see him writhing around on the muddy path, while desperately trying to remove his new problem. He was thrashing around like a mad thrashy thing, which only made things worse, as the netting had wrapped itself around both of his arms now. Riley chuckled as he made his way further up the path, where the next stage of the plan was about to unfold.

Still spinning about like a small whirlwind minus its boots, the stranger had spun himself up the muddy path and was now at the back of and Wiff Waff's shed. And at end of his shed was a slow burning compost heap. It was stacked up with weeds and twigs, and right on the top was a large cluster of old rose stems. On Frupp's cue Burt knocked the whole lot over, right in front of the stranger.

As he couldn't see all that well, the stranger didn't sense that anything was wrong at first. However, as the seconds ticked by, he felt things were becoming more and more uncomfortable and painful on the sole and the toes of his left foot. Done

Without realising it, he was now standing squarely on the rose stems and the prickly thorns were sticking firmly in his foot. He began hopping up down like a mad hoppy thing shouting, "AAARGH, OOOH," and "OUCH," quite a number of times!

Just when the stranger thought that his day couldn't get any worse Ron and Reg pulled the covers off of their acorn machine gun. Rat-tat-tat-tat-tat it went, as Ron pulled the trigger from way up in their fir tree. And, bonk-bonk-bonk-bonk-bonk went the acorns as they bounced off of the stranger's head and body.

Battered on all sides, by the high-speed acorns, the stranger fell over again and the bees were getting ready to play their part in the plan. "Go," Frupp said sharply! And on his command 40 bees flew down and held the stranger's left trouser leg bottom open. They were followed down by 40 more bees who did the same thing to the stranger's right trouser leg.

Now with both targets wide open two larger groups of bees shot up the stranger's trouser legs and stung him on both knees at the same time!

Prior to removing most of rose thorns from his foot the stranger then discovered that he now had a new type of pain to deal with. "OUCH, OUCH," and "OUCHY, OUCH-OUCH," he shouted, as both of his knees began to swell up!

Before the aerial attack had begun, Burt the badger had gone up to the second drippy tap and turned it on. So now the path that the stranger was hobbling about on had become a slippery sloppy mudslide.

Still fighting to free his arms and head from the netting, the stranger slipped over in the muddy mess beneath his bootless feet. Three times he tried to stand up and three times he fell back down. And he was getting muddier and wetter as he did so. It might not have seemed like it at the time but, it was just as well that he had soggy trousers now, as there was one final encounter for the stranger to endure...

A Major upset (Part 3)

...Finally, the stranger found some solid ground to limp about on, up by grandad's shed, but it didn't help him much. Thanks to the work of the bees his knees were swelling up nicely, and he still had a few rose thorns stuck in his foot. He was also covered from head to toe in wet mud now.

At this point Riley was hiding at the back of grandad's shed, where he was laughing and waiting and watching to see how the last part of Frupp's plan played out.

Frupp was standing by Wiff Waff's shed, where his compost heap had been smouldering away for the last few hours. The stranger, who was spinning around like a mad spinny thing again, had spun himself past grandad's shed and neatly towards the slow burning heap.

Frupp took his chance and waddled out into the open. With one swipe of his left branch he sent the stranger reeling towards the smoking pile of leaves and twigs. He spun around one last time, hopped and staggered a couple of times and then sat down right in the middle of the smoking pile!

The stranger paused briefly, finally managing to free himself from the netting but, it was only then that he realised where he was. He just had enough time to remove the last few remaining thorns from his foot, when he noticed he was surrounded by streams of grey smoke and steam. Then, to his surprise, he heard a hissing sound, which was followed by a sprinkling of small flames beneath him!

Still stunned by his experience he muttered to himself, "This can't be right." And after feeling a certain amount of pain creeping up on him, he began shouting, "AAARGH, OOOH, WAHZEROOTY MY BOTTOM'S ON FIRE," then leapt to his feet and jumped straight into the pond!

This was the last time that the gang saw the stranger that day, and they watched as he slopped his way out of the pond and squelched his way back to his car.

"Ha haa, we did it," Riley said beaming from ear to ear, and the whole gang cheered. "I don't think we'll see much of him for a while," he added. What Riley didn't know was, that he would see the stranger much, much sooner than he expected!

After the day's hectic events Riley turned off the drippy tap to save water, sat down and tucked into his snack pack. "So, what have you got to eat," asked Furkitt? "I'm not sure," he replied opening his box. "Looks like a cheese and pickle sandwich, some crisps and an orange drink. "No flies then," Furkitt asked hopefully? "Urrrgh, no," Riley said in disgust!

"So what will you have for your tea tonight," Furkitt asked. "Let's see," Riley replied. "Bangers and mash or toad in the hole I should think." "WHAT," Furkitt said loudly! "You mean humans eat my relatives? I mean, how do you even eat things that go bang, and where do you get the holes from?"

Riley laughed and said, "I'll tell you about it the next time I'm here," adding, "you're lucky you don't live in France mate, they eat frog's legs there!" "Urrrgh, that's not nice," Furkitt said in disbelief, "I shan't be going there for my holidays then!"

Just after 1 o'clock the shed owners returned, one by one, for the afternoon session. Riley said goodbye to Frupp, Furkitt and the rest of the gang and thanked them all for dealing with the stranger. Then he strolled off towards grandad's shed. He wanted to see if there was any more tidying up to do, and ask the other shed owners if they wanted any help.

After clearing up leaves, weeds and some litter for most of the afternoon Riley put it all on grandad's compost heap. The sun was dropping and the blue sky was beginning to turn grey as the clouds began to arrive to cover the whole town of Windowsill Ledge for the night. It was time for Riley to make his way home.

Frupp was waiting in a clump of trees by the three-bar gate to see him off. "Well," he said, "We've had a week of ups and downs haven't we." "We sure have," Riley said. "It's a shame about Loxly, I hope Layla and the cubs will be okay," he added with a sigh. "Don't worry," Frupp said, "We'll look after them."

Just then Layla and the whole gang arrived to say their goodbyes, and Layla was carrying a parcel in her mouth with a note attached to it, which said, To Layla Fox. "What have got there," Riley asked? Dropping it at Riley's feet she said,

“I’m not sure, can you open it and read the note for me please, as I can only read Foxlish?”

Riley undid the parcel and inside he was surprised to find four little yellow waistcoats! The note went onto say, Hope these fit the cubs my wife made them, all the best, The Stranger. “Oh,” they all said bowing their heads in shame, “what have we done?” “We’ll have to say sorry to him,” Frupp said. “I’ll do that,” Riley said, “if I ever see him again that is.”

At that moment the cubs, Basil, Brush, Hannah and Loxly junior arrived and they pushed their way to the front of the gang. Layla scolded them for straying from the den by themselves, but then smiled when she put on their waistcoats, as they fitted them perfectly.

Riley hugged everyone well, except the bees and Norm and his friends that is and said, “Awwww, I’m really going to miss you lot. I’m not sure when I’ll be here again, I’ve got school tomorrow, maybe I’ll see you at the weekends when grandad’s back from his holiday.” Then he waved them all goodbye and slowly made his way home.

When he arrived home, he knocked on his front door and grandad answered it. “Hallo son,” he said with a broad smile, “had an exciting week have you,” he asked? And then gave him a long hug.

“So,” grandad said, “what did you get up to while I was away?” “Not much really,” Riley said shrugging his shoulders. Grandad laughed, “Ha, that’s not what I’ve heard mate, you’d better come in, we’ve got someone here that wants to see you.”

Riley gulped nervously and followed his grandad into the front room. His mum and dad were standing either side of their swivel chair, which was facing the back garden window at the time. But, when it spun around sitting there was the battered, bruised wet and swollen stranger!

“YOU,” Riley said loudly! The stranger just waved and nodded, as he was still in a great deal of pain. “Mum, dad, what’s he doing here, he’s been following me about all week?” Riley asked, standing behind grandad.

He hasn’t been following you, you plum,” grandad said, “He’s been looking out for you.” “But... but,” Riley stuttered. “This is PC World,” his dad said. “He’s a child protection officer at our local police station and he's been making sure that you and the rest of the children in the town have been safe over the holidays. "OH," Riley said really, really loudly!

"What we can't work out," Riley's mum added, "is how you managed to do all of this to one man by yourself?" "Well," Riley said trying not giving the game away, "I did have some help." "Don't tell me," His dad said, "from you imaginary friend?" "Err, yes, that's it, my imaginary friend," Riley said trying to cover his tracks.

"Huh," his mum said, knowing that they would probably never get to the bottom of what actually happened. "Come on," she added, "tea, bath and bed for you mister, you've got school in the morning. And I think that you owe PC World an apology, don't you," she added with a frown?

With a certain amount of guilt, Riley stepped forward to speak to the tired looking PC, as his parents and grandad made their way into the kitchen. "I'm ever so sorry," he said, I didn't know who you were." "That's okay," PC World said, "perhaps I should've introduced myself."

As Riley headed for the kitchen PC World added, "I was glad to hear that the waistcoats fitted the cubs, my son told me." "Yes," Riley said with a grin, "they looked really cute on," as he walked out of the door.

Realising what he'd said Riley peeked back around the door to see PC World winking at him with a knowing smile. Then he thought, "His son - he must have been one of the hunt protesters!" Just then Riley heard his mum say, "Come on you, grandad's going now," and he went to the door to see him off.

"So," grandad said, "you had an exciting week by all accounts." "Yes," Riley replied, "it was much better than being stuck in my bedroom with my X box that's for sure." "Good, I'm glad," grandad added. Just before he left, he said, "Ooh, do me a favour, the next time you're at the allotment, please say hi to Mr and Mrs Twizzy for me will you?" A tired Riley said, "Sure, will do," without thinking, as he watched his grandad disappear up the path waving without looking back.

Riley shut the front door and said to himself, "Hang on a minute, grandad knows Frupp's mum and dad as well, I wonder who else knows the Twizzy Wood secret?"

He went to bed that night thinking about Frupp, Furkitt and poor Loxly and the rest of gang, and was pleased that his secret was safe enough for now. And, even though he had school the next day, he was already busy planning his next adventure at the allotment as he dropped off to sleep...

--- The End? ---

Ingram Content Group UK Ltd.
Milton Keynes UK
UKHW010736280323
419292UK00001B/35